I0385975

MOOCH THE MESSY

An I CAN READ Book®

MOOCH THE MESSY

by Marjorie Weinman Sharmat

Pictures by Ben Shecter

Harper & Row, Publishers

I Can Read Book is a registered trademark of
Harper & Row, Publishers, Inc.

MOOCH THE MESSY
Text copyright © 1976 by Marjorie Weinman Sharmat
Illustrations copyright © 1976 by Ben Shecter

Library of Congress Cataloging in Publication Data
Sharmat, Marjorie Weinman.
    Mooch the messy.

    (An I can read book)
    SUMMARY: Only for love does a very messy young rat
clean up his hole to make his father's visit happier.
    [1. Rats—Fiction. 2. Fathers and sons—Fiction]
I. Shecter, Ben.
PZ7.S5299Mn3   [E]   76-3842
ISBN 0-06-025531-5
ISBN 0-06-025532-3 lib. bdg.

For Fritz

Mooch the rat

lived in a hole

under a hill

in Boston, Massachusetts.

"There is nothing better,"
said Mooch,
"than to live in a hole
under a hill
with a piece of cheese
and a drink
and my own things around me."
Mooch hung his clothes on
doorknobs, lamps,
pictures, and chairs.
He kept his shoes on a table.

8

"What a fine hole

to come home to,"

Mooch always said.

9

One day,

Mooch got a letter.

Dear Son Mooch,

I am coming to visit you
in four days.
I look forward to seeing you
and your hole.

Love,

Father

"Hooray!" shouted Mooch.
"I can hardly wait
for Father to see me
and my hole."

Mooch put one stocking

on a bedpost

for each day that passed.

At last,

all four bedposts

had stockings.

At last,

Mooch saw his father

coming over the hill.

"Father!" cried out Mooch.

"Mooch!" said Father.

They hugged and kissed.

"Come into my hole," said Mooch.

His father looked around.

He saw clothes on doorknobs,

clothes on lamps,

clothes on pictures,

and stockings on all four bedposts.

15

"Mooch," he said,

"you keep a very sloppy hole."

"I like to *see* all my things,"

said Mooch.

Mooch's father

unpacked his suitcase.

"Come," said Mooch.

"I have lots to show you."

"Here is my favorite tunnel.

Scratch those walls.

Scrunch that mud."

"I'm scratching, I'm scrunching,"
said Mooch's father.

Mooch ran ahead.

"Here is my lying-down place,"
he said. "Lie down, Father.
Stretch. Rest."

"I will do all three,"
said Mooch's father.

"Boston is such a fine city
to live under."

"Yes," said Mooch, "there is
so much to scratch and scrunch."

"And trip over," said his father

when they came back to Mooch's hole.

Mooch's father looked around.

"Maybe you could pick up

one coat

or one shoe

or one shirt?" he asked.

"Maybe one thing,"

said Mooch. "Choose."

"I choose a shoe,"

said Mooch's father.

"The one in the middle of the doorway."

21

Mooch picked up the shoe

and put it on a table.

"May I also choose

where the shoe goes?"

asked Mooch's father.

"Yes," said Mooch.

"I choose the closet,"

said Mooch's father.

"I will take away two shoes,"

said Mooch.

"That will make you happier."

"Good boy. Good rat," said his father.

"Now come and see
my cheese tunnel,"
said Mooch. "Sniff!"
"I'm sniffing!"
said his father. *"Mmmm."*

24

"I'm so happy you are here,"

said Mooch,

"to run with

and sniff with

and be with."

25

That night,

while his father slept,

Mooch thought,

"I want to make

Father's visit perfect.

I could start with my bed."

Mooch took crackers, socks,

and cheese wrappers

out of his bed.

"When Father wakes up,

he will see

that I am a neat sleeper."

"Oh, how smooth it feels,"
said Mooch. "How neat.
How horrible!"
Mooch wanted to push and pull
his sheets and blankets.
He wanted to bunch them up
and make little mountains.
But Mooch didn't.
The next morning,
Mooch's father said,
"Your bed lost its bumps!
How wonderful!"

"*All* of today will be great,"

said Mooch.

"I will pack a breakfast

to eat in the field."

Mooch packed

cheese, oatmeal and milk,

snails and sour cream,

and jam sandwiches.

He and his father ran to the field.

Mooch sang,

"I packed a sack.

A sack I packed."

His father sang,

"What did you pack

inside the sack?"

31

Mooch's father bit into a jam sandwich

"Ugh!" he cried. "Ants!"

"Yes," said Mooch.

"I leave my jam jars open.

The ants eat and play

and get sticky and happy."

"Ugh," said Mooch's father again.

"What is a picnic without ants?"

asked Mooch.

"Suddenly I feel full,"

said his father.

"You don't like my picnic,"
said Mooch.

They walked home slowly.

"I will put covers
on all my jars of jam," said Mooch.

"Maybe I'm hungry after all,"
said his father.

He sat down to eat.

"Yikes!" he yelled. "A zipper."

"Sorry," said Mooch.

He put the jacket in the drawer.

"I hope I will remember
where it is," said Mooch.

"When it was on the chair,

I only had to remember

to wear it

when I was cold.

Life was easy."

Mooch's father sneezed.

"Do you have a cold?" asked Mooch.

"No," said his father.

"Dust makes me sneeze."

"Dust is nice to write words in,"
said Mooch.

Mooch's father groaned.

"I think I will go back to bed—
for about a year."

"A year?" asked Mooch.

"Yes," said his father.

Mooch crawled into bed too.

He began to feel sad.

"Dust makes Father sneeze,"

said Mooch.

"So I will get rid of my dust."

Mooch crawled out of bed.

"Good-bye, dust messages,"

said Mooch.

"And Father will feel much better

if I clean *everything*."

Mooch took his belts off the doors.

He took his sneakers off the table.

He took his undershirts
off the lamps.

41

He took his sweaters

off the pictures.

He took piles of sheets

42

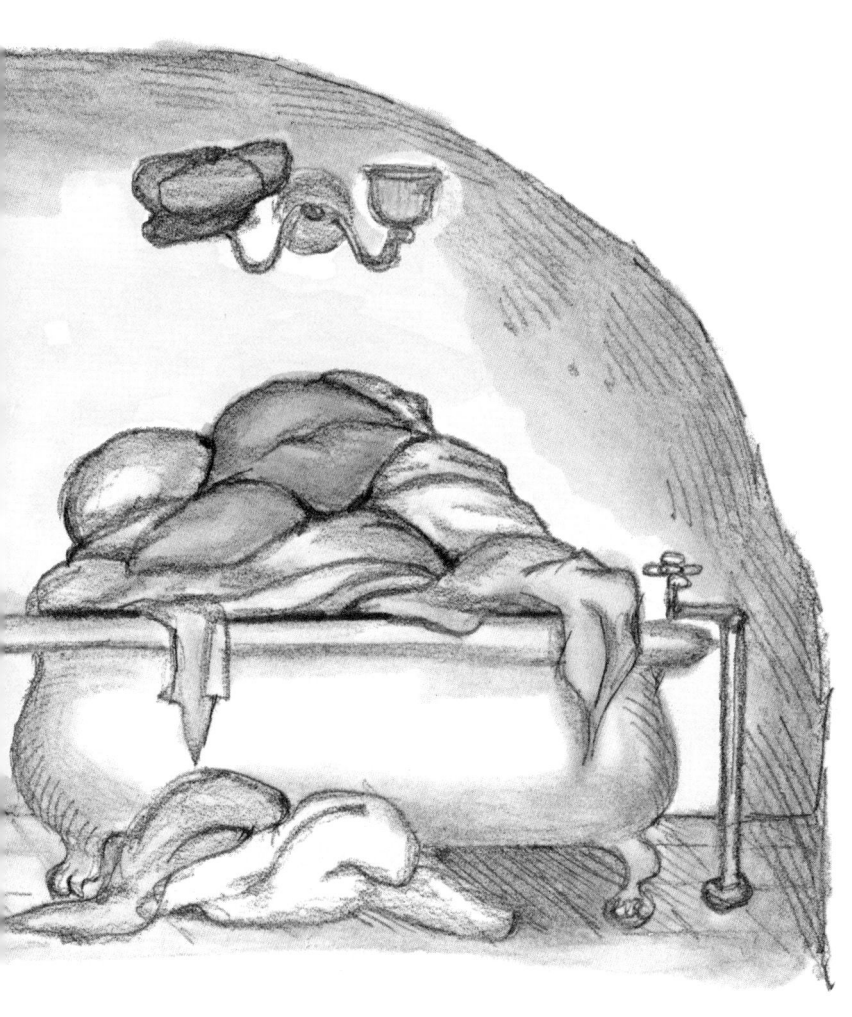

off the chairs

after he took piles of towels

off the piles of sheets.

43

The hole looked very neat
and very empty.
"When Father wakes up," said Mooch,
"he will shout, Neat, neat, hooray!"
Mooch looked around.
"This place looks *too* neat.
I am so mad,
I may tear my hair out.
But where will I put it
if I do?"
He covered his eyes
and he fell asleep.
Suddenly, he heard his father.

"Wake up, Mooch! Wake up!

You have been robbed!"

"Somebody has stolen everything!

Your shoes and sheets

and towels and belts.

Everything that was piled,

dumped, draped, or dropped.

They even took

your dust messages!"

"No, Father," said Mooch.

"*I* did it.

I wanted you to shout,

Neat, neat, hooray!"

"Mooch!" said his father.

"It *is* a neat hole.

Now I really feel at home.

Let's have a good breakfast

and then we can run and run

and scratch and scrunch."

"I'm glad you're happy," said Mooch.

"I love my Mooch!"

said Mooch's father.

"I love you, Father,"

said Mooch.

Many days passed,

and one day

Mooch's father said,

"My son, I am having

a perfect time."

"I don't trip. I don't sneeze.

I don't sit on zippers.

But it is time for me to go."

Mooch helped his father

pack his suitcase.

"I have a good-bye present for you,"
said his father. "Look!"
"A new tunnel!" said Mooch.

"I dug it while you were sleeping,"
said his father.

"Oh, it's dark and muddy
and terrific!" said Mooch.

Mooch and his father

kissed each other.

"I will remember our visit,"

said Mooch's father.

"I am proud of a son
who has his own hole.
And I will remember it
just the way it looks now."
"I'm glad," said Mooch.

Mooch waved good-bye
to his father.
Then he went back
to his hole.

He looked around.

"Neat!" said Mooch.

"I *hate* neat!"

He ran to his closet.

"Hello, shoe," he said.

"Hello, other shoe."

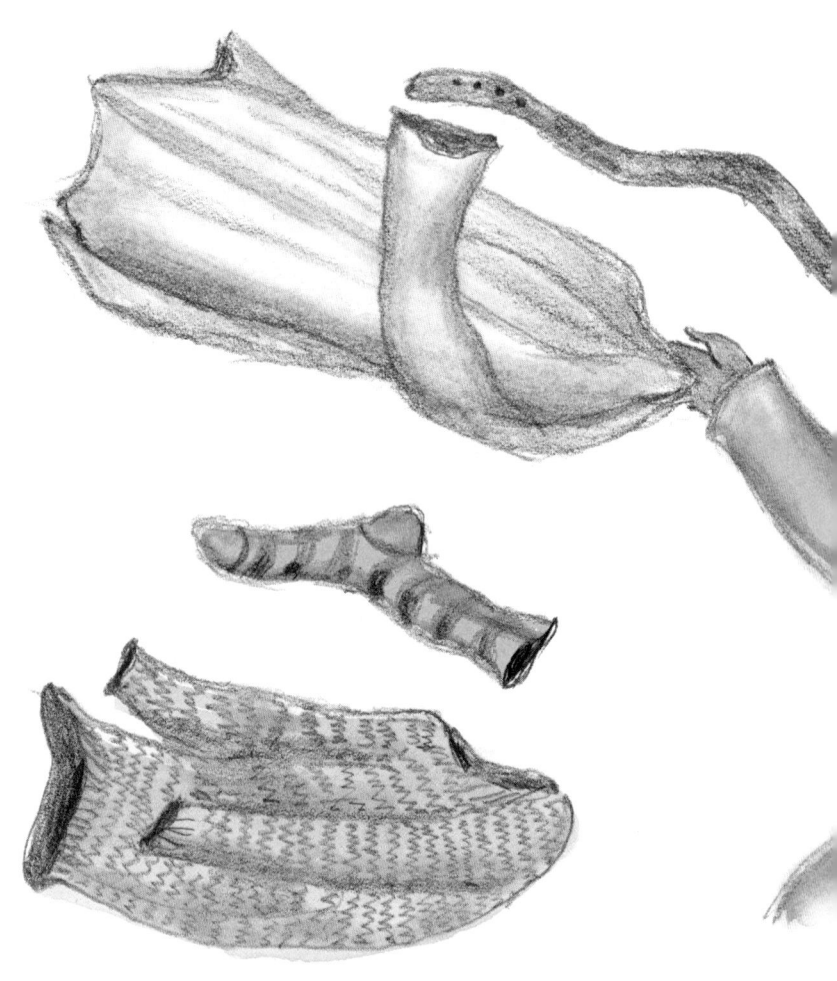

"Welcome home, sock.

Belts, shirts, sweaters,

towels, sheets, blankets,

58

I can see you.

I can see you!

Whee, dust, whee!"

Mooch smiled.

"There!" he said.

"That is the way it was

before Father came."

60

Then Mooch made himself

a cup of cocoa

and bunched up

his sheets and blankets.

Mooch was happy.

"There is nothing better,"

he thought,

"than to be a rat

and live in a hole

under a hill

in Boston, Massachusetts."